YOU'RE MISSING IT!

Written by
BRADY SMITH and **TIFFANI THIESSEN**

Illustrated by
BRADY SMITH

NANCY PAULSEN BOOKS

For Harper and Holt.
Always keep your heads up and eyes open.
There's a lot of beauty out there you don't want to miss.
We love you more than you know!
Love,
Mom and Dad

Nancy Paulsen Books
an imprint of Penguin Random House LLC
375 Hudson Street
New York, NY 10014

Library of Congress Cataloging-in-Publication Data is available upon request.

Manufactured in China by RR Donnelley Asia Printing Solutions Ltd.
ISBN 9780525514428
1 3 5 7 9 10 8 6 4 2

Design by Marikka Tamura. Text hand-lettered by Brady Smith.
The illustrations were done with a #2 pencil, an eraser,
a Faber-Castell artist pen, and watercolors.

Wow!
A big butterfly!
Dad, look!

Ha-ha! The butterfly likes you!

Where's it going?   Let's see.

Look!

The butterfly landed on an egg!

Back to your nest, baby bird.

The butterfly is back!

It's on that funny branch!

See, Dad?

Oh, yes!
I do.
I see.

Hi, butterfly!
Bye-bye, boy!